QREADS

THE EYE OF THE HURRICANE

JANICE GREENE

SADDLEBACK
EDUCATIONAL PUBLISHING

QREADS

SADDLEBACK
EDUCATIONAL PUBLISHING
www.sdlback.com

Copyright ©2010, 2002 by Saddleback Educational Publishing

ISBN-13: 978-1-61651-191-3
ISBN-10: 1-61651-191-5
eBook: 978-1-60291-913-6

Printed in the U.S.A.

19 18 17 16 15   3 4 5 6 7

■ ■ ■

Hurricane Phillip is traveling directly toward southern Florida at this hour. The big storm is expected to reach the coast at approximately 6:33 P.M.," the radio blared.

Laina shifted uneasily in her chair. The three clerks—Laina, Cesar, and Bobby—were taking a break in the back room of Florida Foods.

"I wish he'd shut that radio off," said Laina. "It's getting on my nerves."

Billy Maddox, the store manager, usually blasted music over the PA system. But today there was nothing on but hurricane news.

"Nah," Cesar said. "Playing the radio's

a real good idea. It scares the customers. You know—it makes them panic so they buy more groceries."

Before the store even opened, lines of people were waiting to stock up on food. The three clerks were having their first break in 11 hours.

"Thousands have boarded up their homes and businesses and evacuated. Traffic is at a crawl on major highways as motorists flee the advancing storm."

"Maybe we should get out of town too," Laina said nervously.

"You crazy?" Cesar cried. "You wanna *leave* when Maddox is paying us time-and-a-half for sticking around?"

"Laina—would you feel safer if we went to a shelter?" Bobby asked.

"You're *kidding!* Go to some shelter full of screaming kids?" Cesar butted in. "Nah, this is better. Maddox said we'd be safe out by the loading dock if it gets bad." He put his arm around Laina and stroked her cheek. "Don't worry, babe—I'm here. I'll take care of you." His voice was soft and sweet.

Bobby gritted his teeth. He hated it when Cesar talked to Laina like that. At the same time, he wished he had Cesar's gift for such easy sweet-talk.

Laina pulled away from Cesar. "Okay, I'll stay," she said. "But first I want to make sure that someone drove Tia to a shelter. She said she'd leave a message on my machine." Without another word, she sprang up and headed for the pay phone at the front of the store.

"Forecasters are predicting tides rising up to 13 feet and major flooding in low-lying areas. Governor Hermosillo has declared a state of emergency and called in the National Guard."

Cesar tilted his chair back and fingered the silver chain around his neck. "If Maddox was smart," he said, "he'd jack up the prices. People will pay *anything* right now!"

Bobby stared coldly at Cesar. "Maybe because he's not scum," he said.

Cesar's chair slammed to the floor. "You calling *me* scum, Diaz? Is that what you're saying?" he demanded.

"I'm saying that anyone who would take advantage of people's fear is scum," Bobby said.

"Whoa! *Mr. Saint!*" Cesar said mockingly. "Excuse me for breathing the same air as you! You know something, Mr. Saint Diaz? You know what's good about a thing like a hurricane? It makes things real—like who's gonna survive and who's not. And the ones who survive are the smart ones! It's the law of the jungle. All this polite stuff we do every day—it's not real. The reality is that we're all just animals."

Bobby glared at him. "We're worse. Animals only hurt each other to survive. Only people are greedy."

Laina walked up. "There's no message!" she said in a quivering voice. "I called Tia's neighbors, but none of them answer their phones."

"Don't worry, babe," said Cesar. "Tia's okay.

She probably just forgot to call."

"Do you want me to drive you over there?" Bobby offered.

"That would be great, Bobby! Tia broke her hip last month, so it's real hard for her to get around."

"I'll tell Maddox," Bobby said.

"I'm coming too, babe," Cesar chimed in as he turned to Bobby. His mouth was grinning, but his eyes were hard as flint. "No guy goes off with my baby alone," he added in a low voice.

■ ■ ■

Bobby pulled his car out of the Florida Foods parking lot. The sky was an eerie yellow. Rain was now falling in sheets, blown sideways by gusts of wind.

The traffic was crazy. Cars sped down side streets or crawled along main roads, their horns honking. On one narrow street, Bobby had to pull over to avoid an SUV that was barreling down the wrong side of the road.

It took almost an hour to reach Tia's

neighborhood. Bobby peered through the windshield. "Which way?" he asked.

Laina pointed. "Turn left at the end of the street. It's next to the creek."

The sky was black now. Street lights were out, and every house was dark. Twigs torn from the trees above them slapped against the windows. As they approached the creek, the water on the road rose to nearly a foot.

"Turn around and go back!" Cesar cried out. "This is crazy."

Bobby turned to Laina. "You want to find her, don't you?" he asked.

"Nobody asked you, Diaz!" Cesar snapped. Then he put his hand on Laina's neck. "Babe, your Tia's already left. Look—nobody's around," he said.

"I need to be sure, Cesar," Laina said.

"Let's get out," said Bobby. "We're better off going ahead on foot."

When Bobby stepped out of the car, the warm rain hit him like a shower, soaking him instantly. He stood up, fighting the roaring wind as it whipped at his hair and clothes.

Laina grabbed both his hand and Cesar's. She led them forward.

By the time they reached the house, the water was above their knees. Laina ran up the steps. Wind was whirling through the open front door like an evil ghost. Bobby and Cesar felt their way through the dark rooms while Laina, who knew the house, raced ahead. She cried "Tia! Tia!" But her shouts were carried away in the howling wind.

Bobby and Cesar had returned to the gaping front door when Laina hurried up to them.

Cesar looked irritated. "She's not here, right? Let's go!" he said.

"Let's get to a shelter," Bobby said. "Maybe we can get in touch with her."

The wind was screaming when they stepped outside. Leaves and twigs, propelled by the wind, smacked Bobby's chest and legs. Then a rock hit his face, making him grunt with pain. The force of the wind made it feel like a blow from a baseball.

For a while they walked blindly through the stinging rain. Bobby wasn't at all sure they were headed toward the car. "Let's go back!" he shouted to Laina. But just then, something whizzed by his ear and struck Laina's shoulder. It was a tree branch, as thick as his arm. Laina crumpled and started to fall. Bobby caught her, but Cesar quickly pulled her to his side.

"Over there!" Bobby jerked his head to the left where a dim light was flickering in the distance. The light came from a two-story house. In a few minutes, they waded up onto the porch, Laina stumbling all the way. When Bobby hammered on the door, the light went out. Cesar started to climb through a blown-out window.

"Go away or I'll shoot!" yelled a voice from inside. It was a young voice, high and scared.

"Please help us!" Bobby shouted. "Our friend's been hurt!"

From the window a flashlight beamed out on the three of them. Then the door opened. A boy no more than 11 held the flashlight in one hand and a kitchen knife in the other. Next to him were a younger boy and girl, their eyes big and their mouths taut with fear.

Bobby stepped inside. An inch of water covered the floor. "Give me the flashlight, please," he said. "I want to see where she's hurt."

The children gathered close to Bobby and Laina. "Don't worry. It's not that bad," Laina mumbled.

"Hush," Bobby said softly. "Hold still."

There was a long, shallow cut on Laina's neck. "Do you have a first-aid kit?" Bobby asked the older boy.

The boy nodded and hurried off, splashing through the warm water.

"*I'll* take care of it, babe," Cesar said.

"Let Bobby," Laina said wearily.

As Bobby dabbed Laina's cut with an antiseptic, he smiled at the older boy. "Thanks," he said. "I'm Bobby."

The boy said his name was Ramon. His brother and sister were Michael and

Marisol. They'd been getting ready to leave for the Red Cross shelter that afternoon. A few hours ago their mom had gone to the store to get a few things for the drive. They hadn't seen her since.

■ ■ ■

Bobby made a supper of milk, cereal, cheese, and cold tortillas. Then they made beds by shoving two chairs and a sofabed away from the windows.

Marisol cried herself to sleep. She was sure the roof would blow off the house; no one could assure her that it wouldn't. Bobby dozed and woke, his sleep broken by thumps and whacks as flying objects hit the house.

After an hour or so, Bobby woke up with a start. The wind had stopped roaring, and the air was calm! The sky wasn't black now, but midnight blue. "It must be the eye of the hurricane," he said to himself.

He walked softly to the sofabed where Laina and the kids were sleeping. In the dim light, he could just make out Laina's face.

Suddenly, he imagined Laina sleeping beside him, a wedding band on her finger. It seemed so real, so right, as if he was seeing straight into the future. He reached out—and without actually touching her—his hand followed the soft curve of her face.

He felt Cesar's gaze on him. Cesar said nothing, but Bobby knew he was watching him, and his look was cold. Within minutes the calm eye of the hurricane passed over, and once again the wind began to wail.

It was light when Bobby woke up. The storm was over. Cesar and Laina were sitting on the sofabed. Cesar's arm was around her, and her head was resting against his shoulder. Jealousy burned in Bobby's chest. He stretched out and his feet made a splashing sound! The water in the living room was nearly up to the chair!

"Look!" Ramon said. He and the other kids were standing next to a window. Outside, torrents of water rushed by. The creek had become a river. The house was completely surrounded.

"Look over here," Ramon said as he led Bobby to another window. The house next door had collapsed and fallen into the water. Only part of the kitchen remained, reminding Bobby of an open-backed dollhouse.

Ramon looked frantic. "What are we gonna do?" he wailed.

Bobby turned to the kids. "We're going across the water to higher ground," He said. "Michael and Marisol, you can take one thing from your rooms. Ramon, you gather up anything valuable and put it in a backpack or something. And I need some rope."

The kids took off, sloshing clumsily through the water.

"That's stupid!" Cesar called from the couch. "You're gonna get us all killed."

Laina was annoyed. "Do you have a better idea, Cesar?" she asked.

"Oh that's *nice,* babe—real nice," Cesar said bitterly. He got up from the sofabed and headed upstairs.

Bobby looked out the shattered window. The swiftly moving water was about 20 feet across. There was higher ground on the other side. He could see trees and houses there. Close to the water's edge was a telephone pole. That would be his goal, Bobby decided.

Ramon called out from the top of the stairs, "Bobby? I've got some rope, but I'm not sure if it's okay."

Bobby hurried upstairs. As he passed by the mother's bedroom, a sudden movement caught his eye. It was Cesar, shoving something into his pocket. A jewelry box was open on the dresser!

Bobby was enraged. He charged into the room and yanked Cesar's wrist. A necklace, silver with dark red stones, dropped to the floor.

"They owe us," said Cesar in a low voice. "It's for Laina."

"Laina doesn't want any of your stolen property!" Bobby shouted.

"Shut your mouth!" Cesar cried as he threw a punch at Bobby. Before Bobby could dodge away, Cesar's fist slammed into his ear.

Then Bobby landed a blow on Cesar's

chest. "You're *trash!*" he yelled.

Suddenly, Laina came between them like an angry whirlwind, slapping their arms and shoving them apart. "Stop it! *Stop it!*" she shouted furiously.

"That's Mama's necklace," said Michael in a small voice. The kids were standing at the door, their eyes wide.

Bobby picked up the necklace from the floor. "Ramon, put this in the backpack. Put all her jewelry in there."

Laina turned to Cesar. "You say that you took that for *me?*" she demanded.

"Babe—" Cesar started to say.

"I thought I *knew* you. How wrong I was!" Laina said in disgust.

Bobby turned to Ramon, who was holding a coil of yellow rope.

"Do you know how long that rope is?" Bobby asked the boy.

"I think it's supposed to be thirty feet," Ramon said.

Bobby fingered the nylon line. It looked tough. But was it strong enough for all of them? Then he made a plan. "Ramon, you come across first," he said. "Then Cesar. Michael, you hold onto to Cesar. Laina, you come by yourself, because of your shoulder. You wait, Marisol. Cesar or I will come back for you."

Then he took the rope and hurried downstairs. The water was already washing across the top of the sofabed!

He turned at the sound of footsteps behind him. Laina and the kids stood at the bottom of the stairs.

"How are *you* gonna get across?" Marisol asked.

■ ■ ■

Swim," Bobby said, hoping he sounded more confident than he felt.

"Good luck," Laina whispered softly.

Her concerned expression made Bobby's heart lurch. "I'm gonna imagine your face every minute I'm out there," he blurted out. "That's the only way I'm gonna make it."

He turned away from her startled look

and sloshed to the door.

Outside, Bobby tied the end of the rope to a corner post on the porch. Then he uncoiled the rope, tied the other end to his waist, and jumped feet first into the swirling, gray-brown water.

Bobby was immediately swept downstream. He started swimming, keeping his eyes on the telephone pole. Dozens of household items bobbed in the water—a shoe, a radio, a lamp. Then a tricycle washed in front of him. He fought the current, dodging as many objects as he could. When a thick wooden beam grazed his shoulder, he grunted with pain. Then he ducked below the surface to avoid a huge truck tire. When he came up, a dead dog bumped against his face! He flinched in horror and pushed the carcass away, shuddering at the touch of the wet black hair.

Suddenly, the rope went taut. He was halfway across, but the telephone pole was a long way upstream. So he redoubled his efforts, straining forward against the surging flow.

"Come on! You can do it!" a thin voice called out. An old woman in a jogging suit and house slippers stood on the opposite side. *"Come on! Keep going!"* she yelled, waving her arms frantically.

Then Bobby felt something solid under his feet! Bracing himself against the current, he inched his way along. Whatever it was, the thing that was underwater felt long and solid. Bobby guessed it was a section of roof, or wall—something too heavy to float.

Then the water got shallower, and at last Bobby staggered onto the ground. Gasping for breath, he collapsed face-down on the dirt.

The old woman was beaming at him. "Good for *you,* son!" she cried.

Bobby rolled on his side and smiled up at her.

After forcing himself up, he tied the rope to the telephone pole. A minute later, he saw Cesar start across. Michael was clinging to his neck, his legs wrapped around Cesar's waist.

Cesar moved along slowly, slowly. He

reached out with one arm, lurching alarmingly, as he pulled forward along the rope. Michael held on tightly.

At last they reached the high ground. Bobby saw Cesar panting and shaking out his arms. "You weigh a ton, kid! I think my arms must be about three inches longer now," he joked.

Ramon was next. His thin arms jerked as his body swung left and right, left and right, reminding Bobby of a puppet. But finally, he, too, reached the telephone pole. He dropped in the shallow water, grinning with relief.

"I did it!" he said shakily.

"You sure did!" Bobby clapped him on the back.

Suddenly the rope dipped two feet. Bobby spun around. Across the water, the house was slowly leaning to one side.

"No—" Bobby whispered.

The house stopped moving. Then Bobby saw two figures starting across. Marisol's arms were tightly wound around Laina's neck.

Helplessly, Bobby clenched and un-clenched his fists. He longed to come toward them on the rope—to help them along—but he was afraid the extra weight might pull them down. Then Laina seemed to have stopped moving. Bobby gulped. He didn't want to look, yet he couldn't tear his eyes away.

Michael stood close to him. "Come on, Laina," he said softly.

The sound of footsteps made Bobby turn. A woman with a baby had walked up to join them. The gurgling baby happily kicked its feet.

When Bobby looked back, the house was lurching forward again. The rope dipped and Marisol fell, her arms and legs waving wildly. An instant later, Laina plunged into the water beside her. She snatched Marisol's hair and pulled her close. Then Bobby heard a despairing cry as the young woman and the little girl were both swept downstream.

■ ■ ■

Come on!" Bobby yelled. He ran, racing to get ahead of Laina and Marisol. Not watching his feet, he tripped over a computer printer that had washed up. He landed on a broken fence post that tore his shirt. But he quickly leaped up and ran on.

Ahead, a tall tree had fallen into the water, its branches spread wide. Bobby prayed that Laina could reach it! He could tell that she had also seen the tree. With one arm holding Marisol, she struggled toward the nearest branch.

Bobby scrambled out onto the tree trunk, his feet sliding on the wet bark. Cesar was behind him, yelling, "Laina! Laina! I'm coming, babe!"

"Hold on, kids!" a woman's voice yelled. Bobby glanced behind him and saw the woman who'd been holding the baby. Now she was stumbling forward along the tree trunk. Bobby wondered what she had done with her baby.

Laina reached a thin branch and held on. Marisol gave a hopeful cry as she spotted Bobby and Cesar.

Then the branch began to bend. Laina looked up at Bobby, her lips tight and pale with fright.

Bobby struggled out of his wet jeans, tucked them under one arm, and crawled out along the branches. Twigs bent and snapped underneath him.

Behind him, Cesar yelled, "You're crazy! What are you doing?"

"Don't listen to him! Go ahead now—*Do it!*" the young mother called out.

When Bobby was closer to her, he tossed one leg of his jeans toward Laina. She caught it and held on.

Bobby felt hands on his ankles. Cesar and the young woman were crouched on the branches, holding onto him.

Then they started to pull Bobby backward, an inch at a time. As he moved along the branches, twigs slapped and scraped his bare skin.

"Hang on, kid!" the woman cried.

Laina was slowly, slowly being pulled to the trunk of the tree. At last the woman helped Cesar haul Marisol and Laina all the way out of the water.

The old woman cheered as they made their way back along the log. "You did it!" she called. She smiled at the baby in her arms. "Your mama's a hero, little sweetheart!" she crooned as she handed the child back to its exhausted mother. Then she took some cookies out of her purse. "Here, honey," she said, offering one to Marisol.

Marisol burst into tears. "Thank you," she hiccupped.

Ramon put his arm around his sister, and the woman gently patted her cheek.

"Heroes and cowards," Bobby thought as he pulled on his jeans. "A disaster makes both heroes and cowards."

"Look!" Ramon said in a thin voice. As if pulled by giant hands, the house was breaking apart! First, the walls tore away from the roof. Then the entire second story collapsed. The front door slid into the water, swirled in a circle, and began floating downstream.

Marisol looked desperate. "My whole room is gone!" she wailed.

"Oh, shut up!" Michael snapped. But Bobby could tell that he, too, was trying not to cry.

Bobby drew Michael and Marisol to him. "You're alive," he said, "and you kids still have each other. That's a lot more important than losing *things*. Come on now. Let's get to a shelter and see if we can find your mom."

They said goodbye to the strangers and headed toward Bobby's car. Bobby ached in a half dozen places. Every step he took was painful.

"I'm hungry," Michael whined as they walked along.

"I want to see Mama," Ramon said quietly. Bobby put his arm around him.

■ ■ ■

A brand new pickup suddenly pulled up alongside them. "Yo! Cesar!" a guy called, leaning out the window. Loud music blared from the cab.

"Hey, Kimo!" Cesar called back. "Who you got there with you?"

The driver stuck his head out the window and waved. "Hey there, Ortiz!" Cesar yelled. "What's up?"

"We're taking a drive," said Ortiz. "Why don't you come on with us?"

"Where to?" Cesar asked.

Kimo grinned and winked. "The land of opportunity," he said. "It's all there for the taking." He jerked his head toward the back of the truck. An expensive-looking motorcycle was in the truckbed.

"Cool," said Cesar. "Laina, come on!"

Bobby's heart sank as Laina stepped up close to Cesar. Then she kissed him lightly on the lips. "Bye," she said.

"Chill, babe. All this stuff is just sitting

out there. If we don't take it, someone else will. Come on!" said Cesar.

Laina shook her head.

"Okay, babe, I'll call you," said Cesar.

"Don't call me, Cesar," said Laina.

"What are you doin'? You're saying *goodbye* to me?" Cesar growled.

Laina silently turned away.

"What are you gonna do—hang out with Bobby?" Cesar snarled. "Is that what you want? Bobby only wants one thing from you. I hope you know that!"

"That's enough," Laina snapped.

"I thought you were smart, Laina. Now you're gonna miss out. I'm gonna have all kinds of money, and you'll have nothing! Just don't come crawling back, 'cause this is it! It's over!" Cesar cried.

"Fine," said Laina, but Cesar didn't hear her. He pulled himself into the cab, and the truck sped away.

■ ■ ■

A medicine cabinet from somebody's bathroom had blown through Bobby's rear window. Bottles of shampoo, medicine, and cosmetics were all over the back seat. Laina and the kids cleared the mess away while Bobby tried the engine. After dying twice, it started up with a roar. Bobby sighed with relief.

Just as they were finally pulling away, they saw a military jeep with four armed men in uniform. It swung around the corner and speeded off in the same direction that Cesar had gone.

"Is that the army?" Ramon asked.

"It's the National Guard," Laina said in a soft, sad voice. "They're going after looters."

Bobby looked at her, wondering what she was thinking.

They drove on in silence. Marisol took a Barbie doll out of her backpack and cuddled it drowsily. Michael slumped against her, his eyes closed. Ramon stared out the window, looking worried. Bobby sneaked glances at Laina, who was looking straight ahead. Suddenly, he was feeling shy and embarrassed. He wondered if she remembered the crazy things he'd said to her back on the porch. Why did he tell her that her face was the only thing that would keep him going?

The streets looked as if they'd been hit by a bomb. Bobby steered around a satellite dish, a dead raccoon, a ragged pile of yellow insulation, and a file cabinet. Many houses had no roofs. Some had their walls torn away. Long pieces of metal had rammed into the side of a bus. A tall man with a beard stood on the sidewalk. He was holding a hair dryer, looking exhausted and confused.

■ ■ ■

Finally, they reached the shelter. It was a mob scene. Just to get inside, they waited in line over an hour. Then a white-haired man with a nametag reading "Jimmy" checked them in at a card table in the doorway.

Jimmy's face brightened when he heard Ramon's name. "Ramon *Torres?* Your mother's been trying to get in touch with you!"

"She's okay?" Ramon cried out.

"She was in a car accident. But except for a broken foot, she's just fine," Jimmy said. He turned to a woman behind him. "Beth, could you take these kids to call their mom?"

They hurried away. Ramon's face was wet with happy tears.

Bobby and Laina walked into a large room that was jammed with people. The floor was covered with blue sleeping mats. Some people were sorting through clothes and changing diapers. Others were eating, picnic style, with food spread out on plastic bags.

"Laina!" A tiny woman with a young-old face shuffled up behind them. She leaned forward on a walker, her face lit up with excitement.

"Tia!" Laina screamed. She grabbed the woman in a ferocious hug. "Oh, I'm so glad to see you!" she said.

"Are you okay?" Tia asked.

"I'm fine," Laina said. Then she took Bobby's arm and pulled him forward. "Tia," she said, *"this is Bobby."*

Tia's eyebrows rose. "Oh," she said slowly, her bright brown eyes looking him up and down. "Someone special."

"That's right," said Laina. Her voice was confident and proud.

Bobby's heart swelled in his chest. He made a vow that Laina would always say, *"This is Bobby,"* with the same pride in her voice. Somehow he *knew* he could make that happen.

After-Reading Wrap-Up

1. What does Kimo mean when he tells Cesar that he's headed for "the land of opportunity"?

2. Bobby says that natural disasters make both heroes and villains. What does he mean by that?

3. Why does Cesar call Bobby "Mr. Saint"?

4. What did Bobby, Cesar, and Laina learn from their experiences during the hurricane?

5. What did Bobby see in the eye of the hurricane?

6. What did Bobby use to rescue Laina and Marisol?